Otter B ™
THANKFUL

WRITTEN BY

Pamela Kennedy & Anne Kennedy Brady

ILLUSTRATED BY

Aaron Zenz

Tyndale

Tyndale House Publishers
Carol Streams, Illinois

Otter B: Thankful

© 2022 Pamela Kennedy and Anne Kennedy Brady. All rights reserved.
Illustrations © 2022 Focus on the Family

A Focus on the Family book published by Tyndale House Publishers, Carol Stream, Illinois 60188

Focus on the Family and the accompanying logo and design are federally registered trademarks of Focus on the Family, 8605 Explorer Drive, Colorado Springs, CO 80920.

Tyndale and Tyndale's quill logo are registered trademarks of Tyndale House Ministries.

All Scripture quotations are taken from the Holy Bible, *New International Reader's Version,® NIrV.®* Copyright © 1995, 1996, 1998, 2014 by Biblica, Inc.® Used by permission of Zondervan. All rights reserved worldwide. (*www.zondervan.com*) The "NIrV" and "New International Reader's Version" are trademarks registered in the United States Patent and Trademark Office by Biblica, Inc.®

Design by Mike Harrigan
Illustrations by Aaron Zenz

Text set in Source Sans and Prater Sans Pro.

For manufacturing information regarding this product, please call 1-855-277-9400.

For information about special discounts for bulk purchases, please contact Tyndale House Publishers at csresponse@tyndale.com, or call 1-855-277-9400.

Library of Congress Cataloging-in-Publication Data can be found at www.loc.gov.

ISBN 978-1-64607-041-1

Printed in China

28 27 26 25 24 23 22
7   6   5   4   3   2   1

"VROOM, VROOM, VROOM!"
roared Franklin as he raced
his toy car around the track.

"Look out!" yelled Otter B.
He zoomed his car up a ramp and into the air.
"Whooosh!"

1

"Lunchtime!" called Franklin's mama. She served them hot dog cars with grapes for wheels and celery stick spoilers.

"Yum!" said Otter B. "I can't wait to play some more after lunch."

"Oh, I can't," said Franklin.
"My grandpa is taking me
to the Race Car Museum
to see some real cars."

Back home with Mama,
Otter B dragged his tail.
"I wish I could go to the Race Car
Museum like Franklin," he said.

"That sounds like fun," said Mama.
"Why don't we read your race car
book this afternoon?"

"Nah," said Otter B.
He didn't want to read
about race cars.
He wanted to
see real ones!

That afternoon,
Tabitha came over.

"Hey, Otter B!
I have a brand-new Super Speedy Scooter.
It goes really fast and has sparkly wheels!"

Otter B looked at Tabitha's new scooter.
Then he looked at his. His was not sparkly,
and it had some dents. They raced their
scooters around the block, but Tabitha
went way faster than Otter B.

That night at dinner, when Daddy said the blessing, Otter B couldn't think of anything to be thankful for. He kept thinking about *not* going to the Race Car Museum and *not* having a Super Speedy Scooter.

The next morning, Otter B asked, "Mama, can we go to the Race Car Museum today?"

"No, Otter B. Maybe another day."

"Will you buy me a new scooter?"

"You could ask for a new scooter for your birthday," Mama suggested.

"My birthday is months away!" wailed Otter B.
"I never get anything new. And we never go
anywhere fun!"
Otter B stomped to his room.
He built a tower with his blocks
and then he knocked it down.

"Otter B!"
Mama called.
"Felicia and Roscoe
are here!"

Otter B went outside.

Felicia and Roscoe each had a jar.

"Felicia and I are making Gratitude Jars," said Roscoe.
"Want to make one too?"

Otter B frowned.
"What's a Gratitude Jar?"

"You get a jar and put in pieces of paper with pictures of what you're thankful for," said Felicia. "I already put in that I'm thankful for my dress-up clothes."

"Yeah, and I'm thankful
for snacks!" said Roscoe.

Otter B asked Mama for a jar and
the three friends
started off.

"**Look!**" called Felicia. "**Apples!**" They each drew a picture of an apple on a slip of paper, then put their pictures in their jars.

Something zipped past Otter B's nose. "**A hummingbird!**" he said.

"**Let's put that picture in our jars!**"

16

They spotted a rainbow, a fuzzy caterpillar,
a huge pumpkin, and birds splashing in a birdbath.
When Felicia's grandma gave them each a cookie,
they put pictures of cookies in their jars!

"Hey Mama . . ."
yelled Otter B when
he got back home.

"Come see my Gratitude Jar!"

Otter B dumped out the slips of
paper and told Mama why he was
thankful for each one.

When he finished, Mama smiled.
"You sure seem happier!" she said.

"Yeah," said Otter B. "Once we started finding
all that stuff to be thankful for, I didn't feel so sad
about the museum and the new scooter."

"**AND,**" he added with a grin, "I just thought of one more thing to put in my jar."

Otter B drew a picture of Mama and gave her a big hug. "**I'm really thankful that you are my mama.**"

Mama laughed. "**I'm thankful for you, too!**" she said, kissing the top of his head and tickling his nose.

When you're sad 'cause you can't get

The things you want or see,

Try giving thanks for what you have.

It's how you Otter Be!

Give thanks no matter what happens. God wants you to
thank him because you believe in Christ Jesus.

I Thessalonians 5:18

Here are some conversation starters
to help you talk to your little otter
about gratitude.

Have you ever wanted something, or wanted to do something, but you weren't able to have it or do it? How did that make you feel?

When you couldn't have something you really wanted, what did you do to try to feel better?

Why do you think Otter B started to get happy when he filled his gratitude jar?

If you had a gratitude jar, what are some of the things that you would add to it? Do you want to make a gratitude jar today?

How can being thankful help us to be patient when we are waiting for something we really want?

Sometimes you may feel angry when I say no or tell you to wait for something we really want. What can you do to make that anger go away?

Sometimes when you are angry, you may say or do something that will hurt someone else's feelings. What can you do to show that you are sorry when you hurt their feelings?

Otter B's friends, Felicia and Roscoe, helped him to feel better when he was sad. Who are some of your friends who cheer you up when you are feeling sad or angry?

How can you help your friends or your brothers and sisters when you see that they are sad?

"Hey, Mom and Dad!"

Shaping your child's faith is the most important role you play as a parent. And Focus on the Family cares about you at every step of your journey.

Focus on the Family Clubhouse Jr.® magazine
(Ages 3–7)

A fun, faith-filled publication with puzzles, games, and stories. Subscribe today!

FocusOnTheFamily.com/Clubhouse-Jr-Magazine

As your family goes through each age and stage, Focus is right beside you with trusted, biblically based resources and parenting support.

Encouraged — it's how you Otter Be!

FOCUS ON THE FAMILY'S

pluggedin ®

Help your family make wise choices about entertainment and technology.

PluggedIn.com

And much more at:

FocusOnTheFamily.com/Parenting

LOOK FOR MORE OTTER B™ BOOKS!

If you loved this book, here are more titles with character-building lessons and the fun of Otter B.

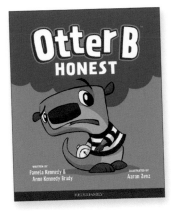

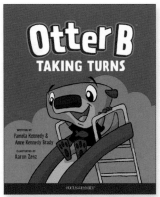

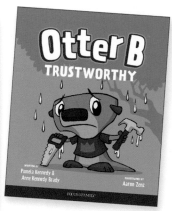

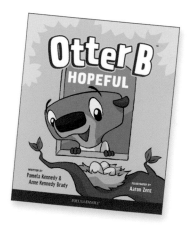

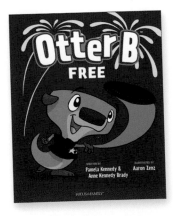

FocusOnTheFamily.com/Store